the **BAD GUYS**

GUYS

EPISODE

• FOR MY BOYS •

SCHOLASTIC PRESS
345 PACIFIC HIGHWAY LINDFIELD NSW 2070
AN IMPRINT OF SCHOLASTIC AUSTRALIA PTY LIMITED
(ABN 11 000 614 577)
PO BOX 579 GOSFORD NSW 2250
WWW.SCHOLASTIC.COM.AU

PART OF THE SCHOLASTIC GROUP
SYDNEY • AUCKLAND • NEW YORK • TORONTO • LONDON • MEXICO CITY
• NEW DELHI • HONG KONG • BUENOS AIRES • PUERTO RICO

FIRST PUBLISHED BY SCHOLASTIC AUSTRALIA IN 2015.
TEXT AND ILLUSTRATIONS COPYRIGHT © AARON BLABEY, 2015.

NATIONAL LIBRARY OF AUSTRALIA CATALOGUING-IN-PUBLICATION ENTRY
CREATOR: BLABEY, AARON, AUTHOR.
TITLE: THE BAD GUYS. EPISODE ONE / AARON BLABEY.
ISBN: 978-1-76015-042-6 (PAPERBACK)
TARGET AUDIENCE: FOR PRIMARY SCHOOL AGE.
SUBJECTS: ANIMALS—JUVENILE FICTION.
DEWEY NUMBER: A823.4

TYPESET IN JANSON, ELO, KERBEROS FANG AND BEHANCE.

PRINTED IN AUSTRALIA BY GRIFFIN PRESS.
SCHOLASTIC AUSTRALIA'S POLICY, IN ASSOCIATION WITH GRIFFIN PRESS,
IS TO USE PAPERS THAT ARE RENEWABLE AND MADE EFFICIENTLY FROM
WOOD GROWN IN RESPONSIBLY MANAGED FORESTS, SO AS TO MINIMISE
ITS ENVIRONMENTAL FOOTPRINT.

17 18 19 / 1

· AARON BLABEY ·

the BAD GUYS

EPISODE 1

A SCHOLASTIC PRESS BOOK FROM SCHOLASTIC AUSTRALIA

GOOD DEEDS.

WHETHER YOU LIKE
IT OR NOT.

· CHAPTER 1 ·
MR WOLF

Pssst!
Hey, you!

Yeah, you.

Get over here.

I said, **GET OVER HERE**.

What's the problem?

Oh, I see.

Yeah, I get it . . .

You're thinking, 'Ooooooh, it's a big, bad, scary wolf! I don't want to talk to him!

He's a **MONSTER**.'

Grandma?

Well, let me tell you something, buddy –
just because I've got

BIG POINTy TEETH and **RAZOR** SHARP CLAWS

. . . and I *occasionally* like to dress up
like an **OLD LADY**, that doesn't mean . . .

. . . I'm a

BAD GUY.

METROPOLITAN
POLICE DEPARTMENT
SUSPECT RAP SHEET

Name: Mr Wolf

Case Number: 102 451A

Alias: Big Bad, Mr Choppers, Grandma

Address: The Woods

Known Associates: None

Criminal Activity:

* Blowing down houses (the three pigs
  involved were too scared to press charges)

* Impersonating sheep

* Breaking into the homes of old women

* Impersonating old women

* Attempting to eat old women

* Attempting to eat relatives of old women

* Theft of nighties and slippers

Status: Dangerous. DO NOT APPROACH

It's all **LIES**, I tell you.

But you don't believe me, do you?

I'm a great guy. A *nice* guy, even.

But I'm not just talking about **ME** . . .

I've got some buddies who have the same problem, so I've asked them to join us.

Any minute now, they'll be walking right through that door.

They're great guys. But just like me, they are **MISUNDERSTOOD**.

So don't go anywhere, OK?

• CHAPTER 2 •
THE GANG

OK. Are you ready
to learn the truth?

You'd better be, baby.

Let's see who's here,
shall we?

Heeey! Look who it is!
It's my good pal,

MR SNAKE.

You're going to *love* him.
He's a real . . .

. . . sweetheart.

METROPOLITAN POLICE DEPARTMENT

SUSPECT RAP SHEET

Name: Mr Snake

Case Number: 354 220

Alias: The Chicken Swallower

Address: Unknown

Known Associates: None

Criminal Activity: * Broke into Mr Ho's Pet Store

* Ate all the mice at Mr Ho's Pet Store

* Ate all the canaries at Mr Ho's Pet Store

* Ate all the guinea pigs at Mr Ho's Pet Store

* Tried to eat Mr Ho at Mr Ho's Pet Store

* Tried to eat the doctor who tried to save Mr Ho

* Tried to eat the policemen who tried to save the doctor who tried to save Mr Ho

* Ate the police dog who tried to save the policemen who tried to save the doctor who tried to save Mr Ho

Status: Very Dangerous. DO NOT APPROACH

Look at this face!
Is this the face of a monster?

I don't think so.

This is **ONE SWEET GUY**.

Will this take long, man?
I've got mice to eat.

Take it easy.
Have a cupcake.

A cupcake?
You got
any mice?

Enough with the mice,
or I'll

EAT
YOU!

goodness,
I wonder who could
be at the door?

Well, well. If it isn't
MR PIRANHA.

Now, if anyone has
a bad reputation,
it's this guy . . .

Hola.

METROPOLITAN POLICE DEPARTMENT

SUSPECT RAP SHEET

Name: Mr Piranha

Case Number: 775 906T

Alias: The Bum Muncher

Address: The Amazon

Known Associates: The Piranha Brothers Gang 900,543 members, all related to Mr Piranha

Criminal Activity:

* Eating tourists

Status: EXTREMELY Dangerous. DO NOT APPROACH

What's *he* doing here?
That guy is crazy . . .

SHHH!

Hey, Mr P!
I know a sweet guy
like you wouldn't say
no to a cupcake . . .

I've come all the way
from Bolivia, hermanos.

And I'm hungry!
So where's the

MEAT?

HA HA!

These guys are killing me!
Always with the jokes!

No meat.

Just cake.

KNOCK!
KNOCK!

AHA!
Now I know
THIS guy likes cake . . .

KNOCK!

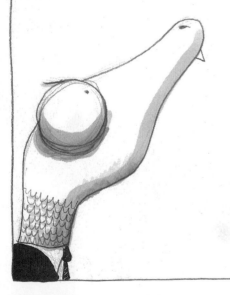

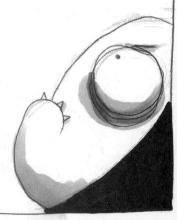

I'm

HUNGRY

You got any seals?

Okey dokey. Nothing to see here . . .

METROPOLITAN POLICE DEPARTMENT
SUSPECT RAP SHEET

Name: Mr Shark

Case Number: 666 885E

Alias: Jaws

Address: Popular Tourist Destinations

* Will literally eat ANYTHING or ANYBODY.

Status: RIDICULOUSLY DANGEROUS. RUN! SWIM! DON'T EVEN READ THIS! GET OUT OF HERE!!

See?! This is what I'm talking about! How will anyone take us seriously as

GOOD GUYS

if all you want to do is

EAT EVERYONE?

What am I **TALKING** about?

Well, sit down and I'll explain.

And that means *you*, too.

· CHAPTER 3 ·
the GOOD GUYS CLUB

AAAiiiEEEEEE!!!!!!

Typical . . .

Hey, shouldn't you two be in water?

I'll be wherever I want.

Got it?

Me too, chico.

See? This is why
I don't work with fish.

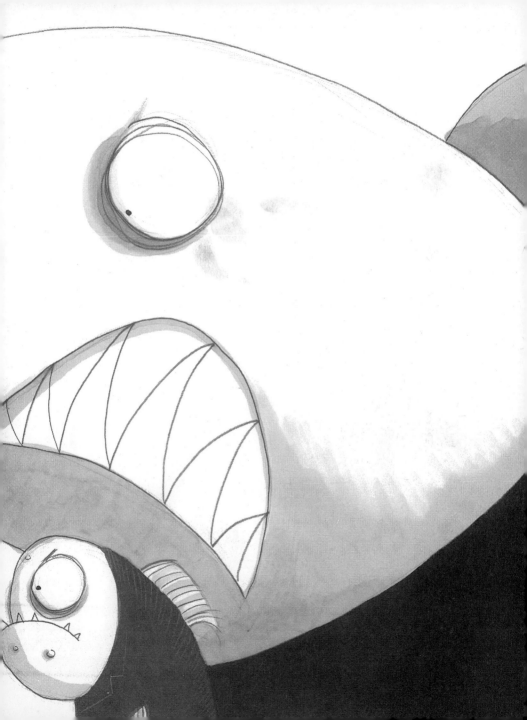

That's
ENOUGH!
We. Don't. Fight. Anymore.

You know why?

Why?

Because **THIS** is the very first meeting of . . .

THE
GOOD
GUYS
CLUB!

That's right!

The

**GOOD
GUYS
CLUB!**

I beg your pardon?

You heard me.

Aren't you tired of being the
VILLAIN?

Aren't you tired of the
SCREAMS?

Aren't you tired of the
FEAR?

Not particularly.

Not in the
slightest.

OF COURSE YOU ARE!

And I have the solution!

POP QUIZ!

Let's say we find a cat stuck up a tree.

What do we do?

You're kidding, right?

This guy's loco.

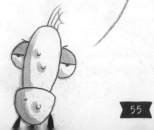

No, I'm not!
I'm a GENIUS!
And I'm going to make us all
HEROES!

He's completely lost his mind.

I came all the
way from Bolivia
for THIS?

You'll be glad you did, Mr Piranha.

And so will you, Mr Shark.

This is going to be **AWESOME.**

Now, **everybody** climb aboard!

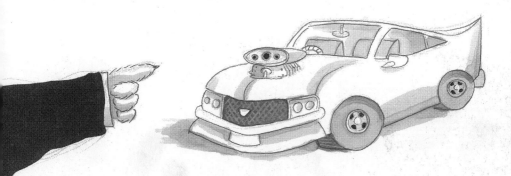

And let's go do some

GOOD!

· CHAPTER 4 ·
CRUISING FOR TROUBLE

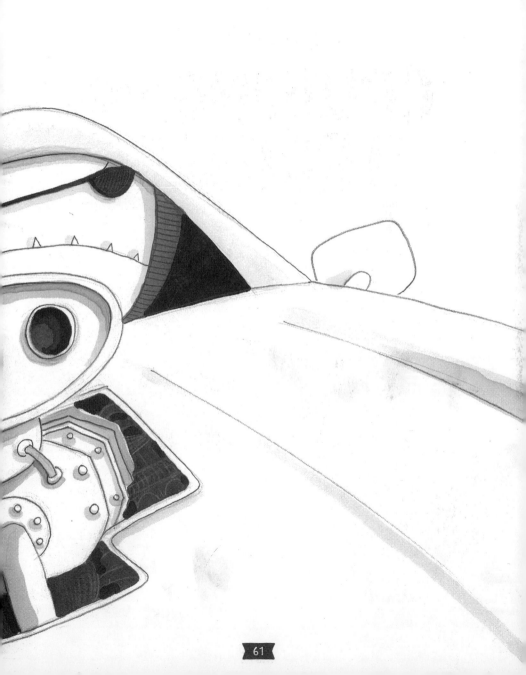

This car is a fuel-injected,

200-HORSE-POWER,

rock'n'rollin' chariot of

flaming **COOLNESS**, my friend.

If we're going to be good guys,

don't you think we should

LOOK GOOD too?

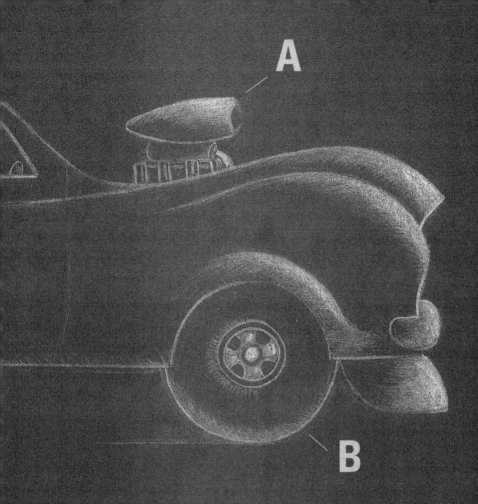

A - 'Fully Sick' V8 Engine that runs on undiluted panther wee.

B - Fat Wheels for just looking insanely cool.

C - Custom Ejector Seats for personal safety and also practical jokes.

D - Oversized Muffler for being very, very loud at all times.

And it's roomy, too!

Hey, it's a sweet ride, chico. But I get carsick, man. So what ARE we doing out here?

We need to
be able to
SMELL
trouble!

In fact . . . wait a second . . .
I think I can smell trouble
right now . . .

Wow, it's really strong,
actually . . .

Hang on. That's not . . .

AW, WHO
FARTED?!

Actually, that feels quite nice.

Seriously though, man . . . what are we looking for?

SCREEECH!

THAT is what we're looking for, Mr Snake!

Meow!

BINGO!

· CHAPTER 5 ·
HERE, KITTY

So, what are we going to do?

Rescue the cat.

And what are we **NOT** going to do?

Eat the cat.

THAT'S RIGHT! I don't know about you, but I feel PUMPED!

OK, now let's do this thing . . .

Meow?

Here, **KITTY KITTY KITTY!**

What was *that*? Are you trying to give him a heart attack?

WHAT? I was, like, being totally cool . . .

Let me handle this.

HEY, YOU!

Get down here, or I'll **SHIMMY** up that tree and **BITE** you on your **FURRY LITTLE BUTT!**

What's the matter with you?!

Well, someone had better do something. That screaming is getting on my nerves . . .

MUNCH!

NOW,

please don't be **alarmed**.

It's true,

snakes can be tricky and they do tend to

swallow things that take their fancy.

BUT – luckily, they swallow them *whole*

and I happen to know a **gentle**,

harmless technique that'll fix this right up.

Excuse me for **one** moment . . .

I SAID . . .

WHERE'S

THE PIRANHA?!

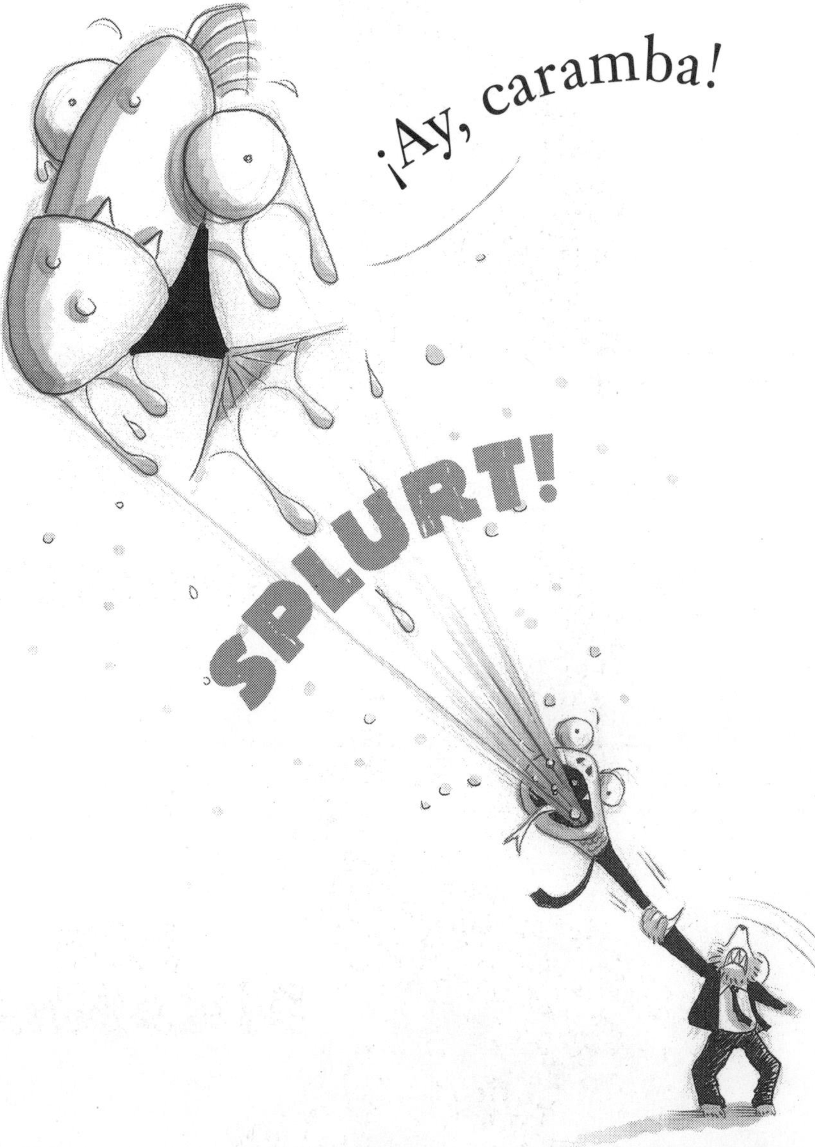
¡Ay, caramba!
SPLURT!

Hey, chico.
What's cookin'?

. . . EOW!

THAT'S IT!

I've got you,
I've got you . . .

· CHAPTER 6 ·
THE PLAN

Nice work.
High fives,
all 'round!

You're the only
one with hands.

Fair enough.

GROUP HUG?

I don't hug. I bite.
So **BACK OFF**,
Mr Snuggles.

Okey dokey . . .

Well, I don't
know about you,
but I'd say we're
READY.

Ready for what?

DOG POUND

20 GUARDS

ONE WAY IN.
ONE WAY OUT.

IRON BARS!
RAZOR WIRE!
BAD FOOD!

There are **200** puppies locked up in the

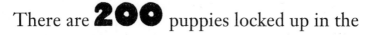

MAXIMUM SECURITY
CITY DOG POUND.

Their hopes and dreams are trapped
behind walls of stone and bars of steel.

But guess what?

We're going to
SET THEM FREE!

We couldn't get a kitten out of a tree. How are we supposed to bust out 200 dogs?

It's easy! One of us just has to get in there and open the cages!

And how do we do that?

With **THIS!**

Are you going to dress up like an old lady AGAIN? It doesn't work, man. You ALWAYS get caught!

Who said anything about *me*?

· CHAPTER 7 ·
THE POUND

Hullo?
Oh, certainly Miss.
I'll buzz you in.

BUZZZ!

Now, what can I do
for . . . uh . . . you?

I'm just a pretty young lady who has lost her dog.
Please, oh please, can you help me, sir?

Well, OF COURSE!

Anything for such a lovely young lass.

Cool.

He's in!
I **KNEW** this
would work.

Now, you know what to do.
Once those cages are open,
we won't have long,
so don't mess it up.

Climb aboard, fellas!

What's that
thing for?

Never you mind. Just hold on tight.
And remember – once Mr Shark
gives me the signal, I'll get you
inside and all you have to do is tell
the dogs which way to run.

GOT IT?

Yeah. But
how do we
get inside?

But don't worry!

I have **EXCELLENT** aim

and I'm **85%** sure

that I'll get you in on my first throw –

THAT'S

how confident I am!

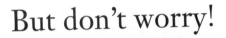

You know, I wouldn't normally open all these cages at once, but since you asked so nicely . . .

Well, here's the last cage. Is THIS your dog?

There's no time to talk! Hold on tight, little buddies.

It's time . . .

to go
BE A HERO!

SWOOSH!

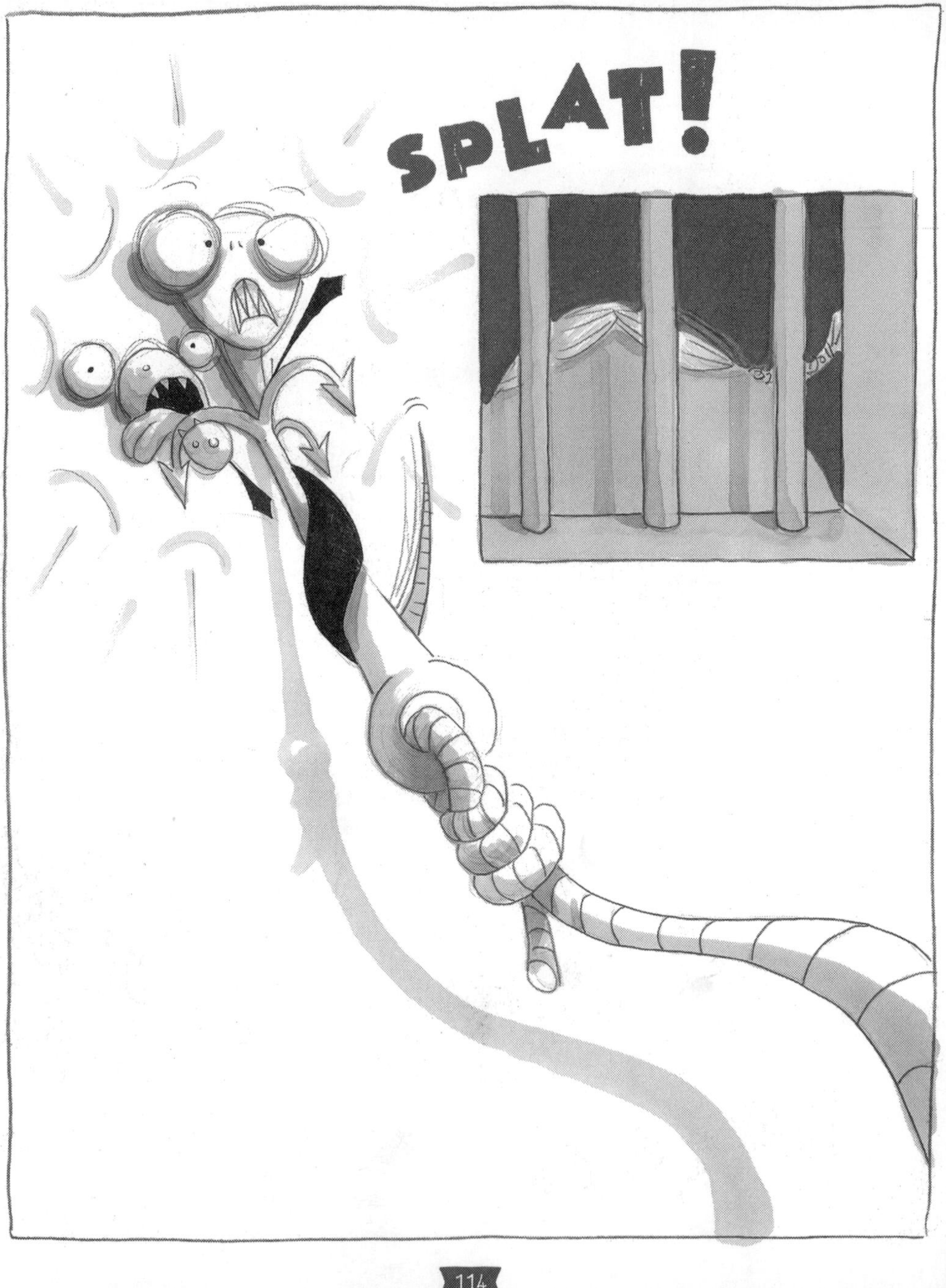
SPLAT!

OK.
Best out of three.

YEAH.
I'm getting the
hang of it now . . .

SPLAT!

SPLAT!

SPLAT!

SPLAT!

SPLAT!

I'm sorry, young lady, but I'd better lock these cages back up now.

THIS. IS. GOING. TO. WORK.

If we survive this, I'm going to *eat* that wolf.

WHOOOOSH!

Not if I do first.

OK, fellas!
Back in your cages.

We're **NOT** going to make it.

We're **NOT** going to make it.

We're **NOT** going to make it.

We're **NOT** going to make it.

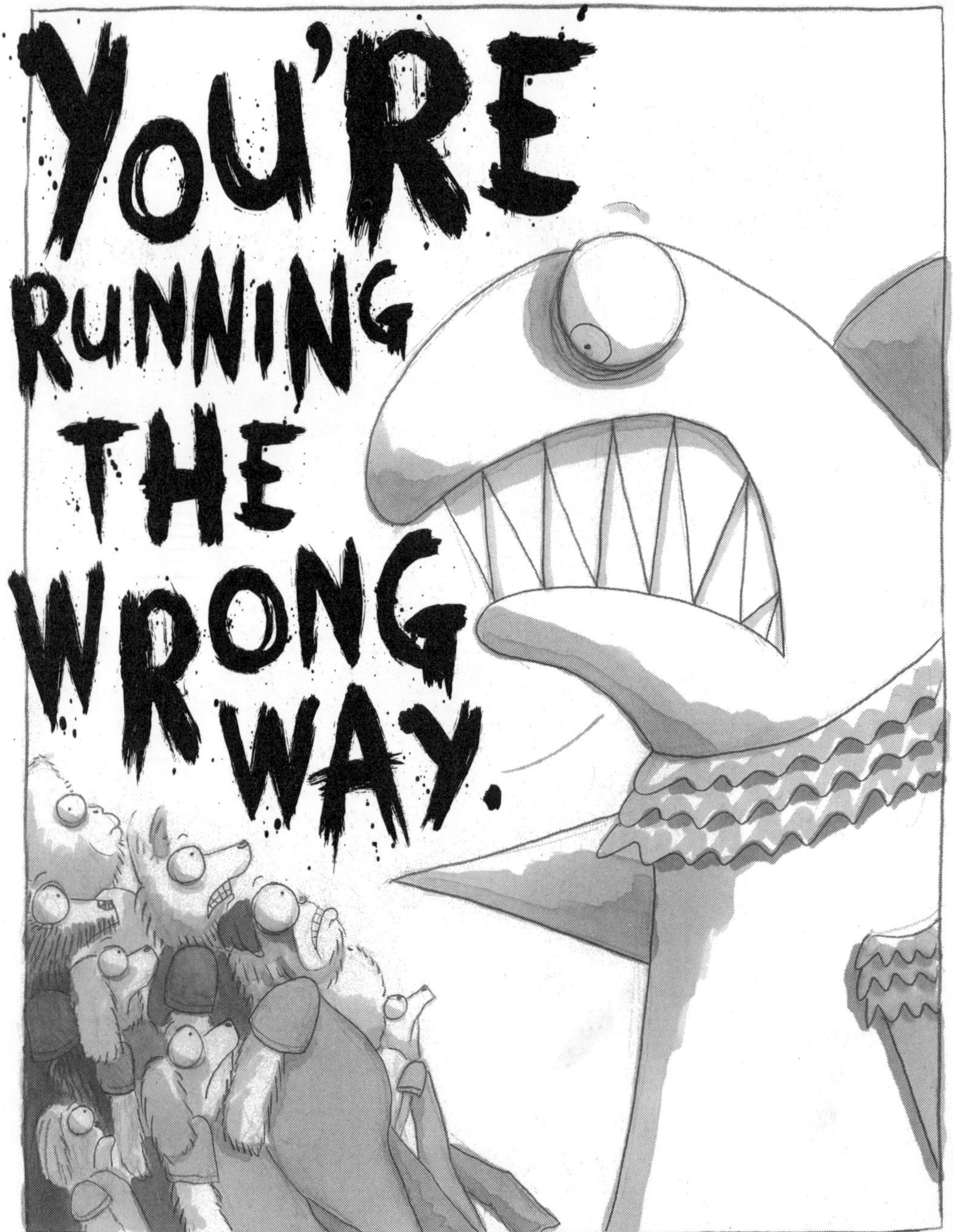
YOU'RE RUNNING THE WRONG WAY.

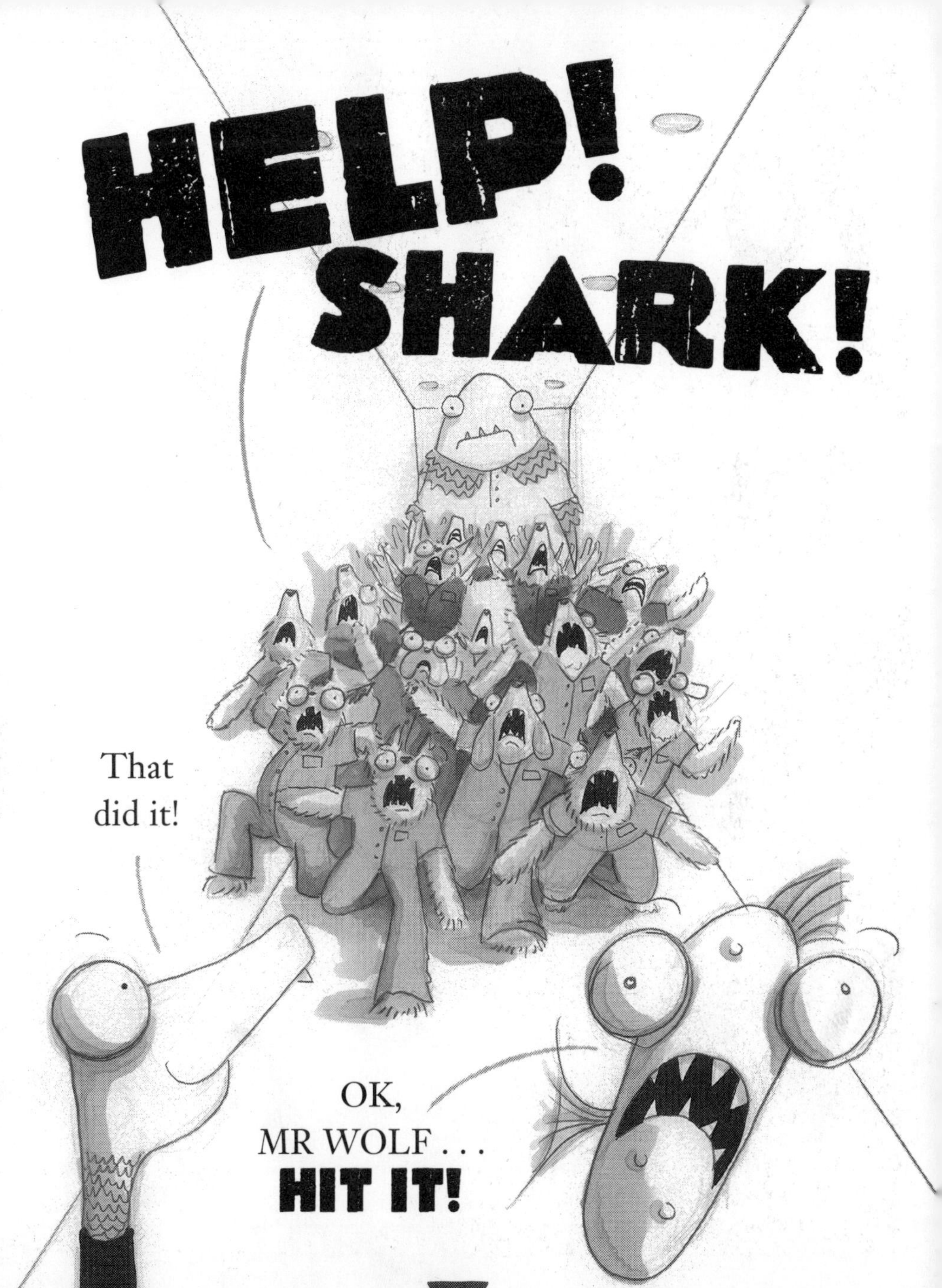
HELP! SHARK!
That did it!
OK, MR WOLF . . . HIT IT!

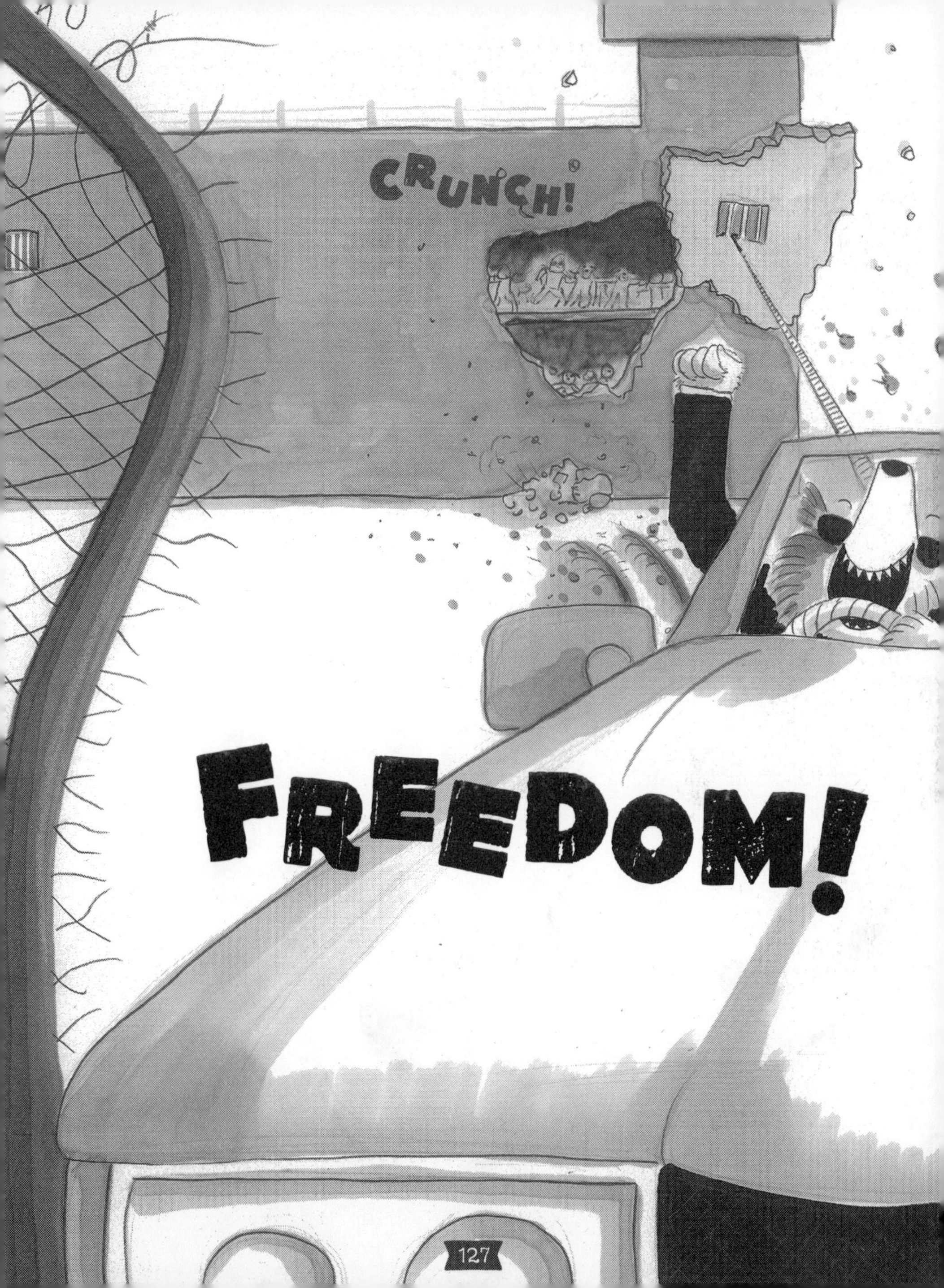
CRUNCH!
FREEDOM!

Look at them, guys! We've **changed** their lives! And they'll **love us** FOREVER!

HELP! A **WOLF!**

128

· CHAPTER 8 ·
SO, HOW ABOUT IT?

Well, they certainly didn't seem very grateful, did they?

They called me a SARDINE!

I thought you WERE a sardine.

I'm not a SARDINE! I'M A PIRANHA, man! **PIRANHA!**

Whatever.

You're missing the point, guys. **WE DID IT!** We gave 200 dogs a whole new life. Doesn't that just make you feel **AWESOME?!**

You really do hug WAY more than I'm comfortable with, man.

Aw, **C'MON!**

You loved it! I KNOW you did!

Tell me the truth – didn't it feel great

to be the **GOOD GUY** for once?

Tell me how it felt, fellas . . .

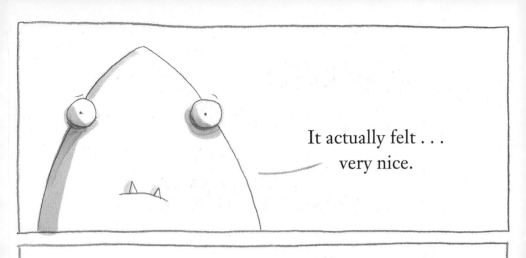

It actually felt . . .
very nice.

It felt better than nice.
It felt . . . good.

It felt **WONDERFUL**, man.
But they still called me a SARDINE!!!

If you stick with me, little buddy, no-one will mistake you for a sardine ever again! You'll be Bolivia's most famous hero! Are you with me?

Sure. But you'd better be right, chico.

And what about you, big fella?

I . . . I really liked being good. I'm in.

That just leaves you, handsome. What do you say? Want to be in my gang?

Only if I have your word that there'll be no more hugging.

I'll try, baby! But I'm not making any promises!

Today is the first day of our **new** lives.

We are **not** Bad Guys anymore.

WE'RE
GOOD GUYS!

And we are going to make the
world a **better** place.

For the first time in my life . . .
the future smells sweet!

Wait a second –

That doesn't
smell sweet . . .

Piranha, did you
fart *again*?

I get gassy when I'm
upset. Just deal with
it, chico.

TO BE CONTINUED . . .

GUESS WHAT?

The **BAD GUYS** haven't even warmed up.

Freeing 200 dogs is **NOTHING**.

How about rescuing **10,000 chickens** from a **High-Tech Cage Farm** protected by the world's most **unbeatable** laser security system?

BUT how do you rescue chickens when one of you is known as **'The Chicken Swallower'?**

Join the **BAD GUYS** when they return for more dodgy **good deeds** with a new, creepy member of the team . . . and keep your eyes peeled for the **SUPER VILLAIN** who just might be the end of them.

EPISODE 2
COMING SOON!